THE MIGHTY
MARATHON

THE

MIGHTY

MARATHON

by William Cramer

This book is a work of fiction.
The names of the characters and the events in this story
are a part of the imagination of the author.

The author would like to thank Erik Weihenmayer and Louie McGee, for making him aware of their athletic ability and their service to others who are visually impaired. Thanks also go to those in the bibliography for their contributions to the scope of the running world.
Finally, the author would like to thank Gregory Ruffin for all his guidance in preparing him for a half-marathon.

I dedicate this book to Gregory Ruffin,
the kind of friend who inspires you every day.

TABLE OF CONTENTS

Introduction...9

Chapter 1...11

Chapter 2...17

Chapter 3...23

Chapter 4...31

Chapter 5...39

Chapter 6...47

Chapter 7...55

Chapter 8...63

Chapter 9...67

Bibliography 73

About the Author 74

Introduction

Over a hundred thousand people on this planet run in a
marathon every year. I have to ask the question, why?
Why do they choose to undergo all they must endure getting
to the finish line? The answer to that question is change.
They want some type of change to take place
in their life.
If they're running for fitness and health, it's change.
If they're running to improve their social status,
it's change.
If they're running for personal growth, it's change.
If they're running to relieve stress, it's change.

**If you are seeking change through the running
experience, this book is for you.**
It talks about: Moving forward • Setting goals •
Mind over body • Admitting your fears
**If you want to learn about running in marathons,
this book is for you.**
It talks about: Bib colors • Runners pack • Pacers in
the race • Starting line flags • Recovery stations •
Planning for the finish line • Tracking the runner
**If you want to learn how to improve your running game
this book is for you.**
It talks about: Carb-loading • Running style • How to pace
your race • Energy gels and chews • Visualization: the mental
game • Eating clean

WILLIAM CRAMER

Chapter 1

Running a marathon was Mr. Ruffin's idea. He had started off running half-marathons and before you knew it he was running full marathons. He would always say, "How many people do you know run marathons?" When I thought about it I realized Ruffin was the only one. I started running about three years ago. I would set a goal on how far to run during the summer, and use my Under Armour app to track the miles.

I never thought about running a marathon until Ruffin said one day, Cramer all those miles you run each week, you could run a marathon. I did run a lot of miles each week.

I laughed as I drove home thinking about what he said in

class. He was the high school gym teacher, and as a fellow teacher we often talked about what we did outside of school. That night I met up with some of my friends, and we were having a drink talking about our lives. I mentioned that I was thinking about running a half-marathon that was coming up in Baltimore. They all started laughing. Myra spoke up quickly and said I'm running that marathon next month. Courtney high fived Myra and said I'll run it with you.

Myra was short, around 5 foot 2. She had more spirit than Joan of Arc, but she was a girly girl. She was thin with short brown hair, always wearing the latest styles. She designed clothes for an overseas company.

Courtney worked at a local gym as a trainer. She had a few kids, and she was thin and tall. She liked her workout gear, and she always wore her Apple Watch to keep in touch with her clients. Her favorite pastime is shopping online and working on her six-pack, that was on its way.

Another one of my friends, Larry who never ran that much for exercise or even pleasure spoke up and said to the girls, Cramer and I will run the marathon too. I looked at Larry and said we are going to run a marathon? I mean I have been thinking about it but you're going to run one with me? Larry looked at me and said of course Cramer.

Larry was a car salesman, he was used to sitting at his desk, chunky from all the vending machines at the dealership. He was respected by all, he was the top car salesman at that dealership for the past 10 years.

Larry had long brown hair, blue eyes and snow white teeth. Larry had liked Myra for a long time, he never had a chance to connect with her but the marathon would be the perfect opportunity. The deal was sealed before I could say a word, all four of us were going to Baltimore to run the half-marathon.

As we left the Brewery it was dark, there were a few street lights shining on the small town streets. Some local mom and pop stores were closing. We ran to our cars laughing and shouting I won the race. It was in that moment that I felt the excitement of the race and I yelled out at the top of my voice, I'm in, I'm running that damn marathon.

The next morning I told Ruffin in the hallway that I signed up for the half-marathon in Baltimore. Quietly, he just looked at me and with his rough voice said, cool man. I didn't expect too much, after all running a marathon was old news to him.

A week went by and we all got together at the Brewery to have a few drinks again like always. Some of us started talking about looking for a place to stay in Baltimore. Myra said she booked a room at the Holiday Inn Express and suggested we do the same. Larry leaned over to me and said that place sounds perfect, let's stay there too. He booked us a room later at the same motel. The rest of the night we talked about the race.

That weekend we all got together to go shopping for running clothes. It was a whole day's event. While we were shopping I said to Larry, what do you call men's yoga pants? He laughed uncontrollably, and almost fell over some displays in the sporting goods shop. They are called compact pants. Oh, OK I need some for the race because it's going to be a little cold on race day.

The girls met up with us and we all went to get something to eat. Larry and Myra were getting along so well I almost forgot that he was trying to connect with her because it seems that he was there right where he always wanted to be, next to Myra.

While we were eating, Larry and Myra were laughing together sharing food and drinks. I could hear music in the background playing at the restaurant. It was Prince singing, "You don't have to be rich to be my girl, you don't have to be cool to rule my world, ain't no particular sign I'm more compatible with, I just want your extra time, and your....... Kiss."

I looked at Courtney since she was laughing, catching her eye I pointed at the happy couple with my own eyes. She nodded her head and continued to laugh. I felt that she had known something was up about Larry and Myra for some time. It wasn't just Larry that liked Myra, Myra liked Larry also. Of course, Courtney was keeping it on the down low.

That night I lay in bed laughing. I couldn't get that damn song out of my head. It's exactly what Larry ordered. Extra time, and a kiss from Myra. Myra was worth waiting for because she was solid. She had her life together. She was kind and she knew what she wanted to do in life. Ask yourself how many people do you know like that? They are far and few between.

I guess we all had different motives for running the marathon, but for me, it was on my bucket list, I just didn't have the guts to do it until Mr. Ruffin brought it up. I had thought about it a few times over the past few years but I never signed up for one. Putting my last daughter through college, I finally felt free to focus on myself. I knew the window of opportunity to fulfill my bucket list before I got old was small, so I fast-tracked it. I worked on multiple goals at once. I put together a workout plan to run each week, and before I knew it the race was here.

I asked Larry if he was ready to run the marathon. Larry said he was more than ready. He was going to follow Myra all the way to the finish line. I saw Courtney running while going to pick up some groceries, she wasn't messing around. I couldn't tell you how fast she was running but her pace was brutal. She was an athlete in high school, and knows how to train.

I felt ready for the marathon too. I had been running for the past 3 years. I started off running 3 miles, then 6, and now was up to nine miles each time I run. I tried to run ten or eleven minutes per mile. Believe it or not, that is really not that fast at all. I figured if I kicked up my distance to ten miles for a month I would be able to make it to the finish line.

I have to be honest, I was a little afraid. I had two fears. My first fear was I didn't want to end up in last place. The second fear was I didn't want to get lost during the race, so I wrote all the streets for the course down on my hand. OK I know it sounds corny but I wanted to be prepared for the worst. I imagined running the course and getting lost somewhere and I didn't want to ask someone for directions. How crazy would that sound? Excuse me sir...... I think I'm lost. My bottom line was, all I had to do was beat myself, and I needed to know where I would be running in order to do that.

The next day all four of us were going to Baltimore, we were talking about what we expected to happen during the race. It's funny how we sometimes talk when our expectations don't match our abilities. When there are twenty-thousand people running the race and you expect to be in the top ten percent.

I turned to Larry and said really, Larry how can you say

you will finish in the top ten percent. Do you mean the bottom ten percent, cuz that number sounds real? We all laughed but Larry changed the subject and started talking about the new shoes that would take him across the finish line. Myra laughed and looked at him and said Larry I will be taking you across the finish line myself. Wow, Larry it looks like the cards are stacked in your favor. It sounds like all you have to do is show up.

Myra and Courtney started talking about their new running outfits, and about the excitement of doing something different. Of course, Myra is always pushing that designer stuff, but that's not how Courtney rolls. Courtney loves that sports stuff without the fringes.

Chapter 2

We all met at my house early in the morning. Larry had one suitcase, I had one suitcase but the girls had several each. I said to the girls you realize we're only going for the weekend. Myra said funny Cramer but we got stuff we need to bring. Make sure there is some room cuz we are going to bring it all. Larry do you have any ideas on how to put all this stuff in my trunk? Larry said yes, so I let him work his magic, and soon we were on our way. The girls were texting their friends saying they were going to cross the finish line before us. They both shouted out loud at the same time, hey guys we told everyone that we're going to cross the finish line before both of you. Larry and I laughed and said that was a bold move, but it will never happen.

I said let's make it fun, whoever loses pays the motel

bills. They said no problem we got this, we will both beat both of you. We stopped for coffee and then continued on to Baltimore. The girls were on FaceTime with their friends, while Larry and I started talking about cars.

After three hours driving, we were ready for a break. Everyone was saying are we there yet? I said we will be there in a while but let's take a break. We stopped at a roadside rest. We went to the bathroom and tossed a Frisbee around for a few minutes. We got back in the car again headed for the Holiday Inn Express. Does anyone else even play Frisbee anymore? I've got to ask around.

We got to the motel early and checked in, the motel was right beside a 7-11. It was also in walking distance of the Inner Harbor where we would line up to run the race in the morning.

Larry and I shared a room next to Myra and Courtney. After putting our luggage in the room we were off for some food, and down to the Expo to pick up our race packets. Race packets are important. It's not like you can do without them, and there is a limited set time they give you to pick them up. So we hurried up to head to the Expo for our packets.

We all have this perception of what a marathon runner looks like, but there was a kid in the motel elevator that was running the half-marathon. He looked to be around 10 years old. Larry laughed when the boy told us he was running the half-marathon.

I was thinking wow, what was I doing when I was 10 years old. I wasn't thinking about training to run a marathon. I think I was playing with Lincoln Logs.

While I was deep in thought the elevator door opened and I stepped out with the boy, Larry wasn't looking where he was going and he fell flat on his face. Karma is a loop, what we send out does come back sooner or later, in this case, it was sooner.

I helped Larry up from the floor worried that my friend was hurt. I said, Larry what's going on with you, laughing at him. I should have left you on the floor.

Larry said he knew I wasn't making fun of him I just didn't see the kid on the same level as I'm on now. Well, Larry, he could be on the same level as you. Just because he is small doesn't mean he can't run faster than you. Look at Myra, have you seen her run at all.

Larry though for a moment and then said no. Ok, Larry wait till you see her run in the marathon. She is fast and she holds several high school and college records in the two miles. Do you even listen to what she is saying when we go to the Brewery to hang out each week? Well, to tell you the truth I'm usually captured by her beauty. That's cool but you can't spend the rest of your life in that mode. You have to move on to hear what she is saying when she talks. How will you really get to know her?

When Larry makes a mistake instead of owning up to it he keeps digging a bigger hole. We have been together since the second grade, we learned how to ride bikes together, and we played football together in high school. He is one of the funniest persons on the planet, almost as funny as Redd Foxx was.

He used to live across the street from me when we were in middle school. When he wanted to play he would run around to our back sliding door and put his face up against the window. That's where our kitchen table was, and we were usually eating dinner. My dad would look at him and start to laugh. His sister Diane used to do the same thing. I guess that's why my family fell in love with them. They were a huge part of our family. Larry is one of those friends that you hate and love at the same time. Do you know what I'm talking about?

We made our way out to the front of the motel to get a ride, and a cab picked us up and took us down to the Harbor. We jumped out of the cab and started to look for a place to eat when we spotted a Chick-fil-A fast food restaurant that was right down the street from the Expo. Larry said let's hit it, I love those fries and we walked across the road to eat some chicken.

Right before we got to the door of Chick-fil-A we saw a homeless woman around our age sitting against the wall next to the restaurant. I thought she might look up and ask for money but she didn't even make eye contact. She was wearing yoga pants, a green army jacket, gloves, a blue scarf and a pullover hat with her hair tucked up into a bun. There were a few strands of hair hanging down each side. She was only wearing socks no shoes. As we approached she leaned forward reaching into her backpack, she pulled out some crackers and said, are you guys hungry?

I didn't say a word but Larry with his quick humor said to her you had me with hello. She bounced up and said to Larry, what are you waiting for? Are you going to carry me out of this mess like Jerry Maguire? Larry replied, yes Dorothy I'm finally here.

She had such an awesome personality, and she was as bright as the Cape Hatteras Lighthouse on Hatteras Island. They say you can see that light 20 miles out to sea. I'm not sure about that but you understand what I'm trying to say. When she reached out to shake my hand I could feel her energy. I often see homeless people on the streets and wonder what it would be like to have a conversation with them. I had so many questions that I wanted to ask but especially, how does a person become homeless?

Do they wake up one morning and say today I'm going to be homeless and live on the streets? The pain of getting up, getting ready, driving to work, trying to do your job each day sucks, but in light of all that, does being homeless suck less or more? I think of all the clothes I have to wash and iron. The house I have to clean each week. The appointments that I have to go to each month. Maybe just doing nothing at all would be better. After all the grass grows back each week and I spend my paychecks on bills, so what's the point. Maybe they have it right and we have it wrong.

There was Dorothy, which is not her real name, talking to us outside Chick-fil-A. It was exciting but awkward just standing there when no one was talking so I said to Dorothy, would you like to eat with us at Chick-fil-A?

There was a moment of silence before she said yes. She started to pull out some change and count it, but I quickly looked at her and said, Dorothy, it would be an honor to treat you to a meal. Besides, I have a ton of questions that I would like to ask you.

Larry spoke up and said that would be awesome if you would eat with us, we're from out of town and it would be great to met someone from Baltimore. I wasn't sure what it would be like, eating with her, but I was intrigued that she would give us a moment of her time.

We got our food, sat down to eat, and chatted a little. We talked about our favorite food, of course I had to share my chicken noodle soup and apple pie recipes. Larry talked about his mac and cheese sandwich, and Dorothy shared some of her favorite foods to eat. Dorothy asked what we're doing in Baltimore and we told her that we were here to run a marathon. She lit up when we said marathon, she loved watching them each year, and always wanted to run in one someday.

After we ate Larry said we are going over to the Expo to pick up our runners package, why don't you tag along? She said really, that would make my day. Sometimes I watch runners go into the Expo and come out but I am always afraid to go in and look around. Larry said to Dorothy it's time you took a look around the Expo to see what you have been missing.

Chapter 3

Across the street and into the Expo we went viewing all kind of vendors of sporting goods and food. Vendors give you lots of free stuff like shirts, food, drinks, pens and novelties to take with you. We loaded up on everything, placed it all in a large vendor's bag and handed it to Dorothy. She laughed and said thanks, but I think that it's more than I will need for a long time. I usually travel light, I live day by day. Whatever comes my way comes.

I was thinking of my bank account when she was talking, I kind of live day by day too. On a teacher's salary, I seldom have extra money to put into a savings account or buy stocks or bonds. The only difference is that at the end of the day I worry about money and Dorothy doesn't.

Viewing all the vendors with their running gear, and watching all the athletes move throughout the Expo creates excitement, revolving around the Marathon.

Dorothy was talking to one of the vendors and expressed her desire to run a marathon, Larry and I chipped in and asked if she would like to enter the race tomorrow. She said she yes so we signed her up and bought her some shoes. Dorothy was going to run the half-marathon with us.

She sat down on the floor and put on the running shoes. She looked at them and said they feel awesome. I said stand up and walk in them. Larry and I grabbed her hands and pulled her up.

She kept walking around in circles until she got dizzy. Ok, Dorothy how do they feel now. Dorothy said I feel like I have wings. I said cool, when I wear my Under Armours I feel like someone is pushing me all the way to the finish line. All three of us laughed.

We left the Expo and told Dorothy we would see her in the morning at the starting line. Larry and I got a cab back to the Motel to catch up with the girls. Larry and I both talked about Dorothy on the way home, there was something different about her that neither of us could figure out. Here is a women homeless, highly educated with great social skills, and in great shape sitting on the street with old clothes and no shoes. She must have traveled a lot because she expressed a magnificent understanding of places.

The girls picked up their runners package which includes a map to the half-marathon, your bib number, marathon shirt and start time for all the races. They also introduced us to some ladies they had met in the lobby. Their names were Patti and

Stephanie from New Jersey.

Patti and Stephanie were good friends. They drove to Baltimore this morning and arrived about the same time we arrived. They were both going to run the half-marathon with us on Saturday. Patti had a few kids coming in the morning to cheer her on, she was around fifty years old and she was in decent shape. She did go out for a smoke break while we were talking, with a cup of coffee she got next door at the 7-11.

Stephanie was in her sixties, she had long grey hair, and was more muscular than any bodybuilder on the cover of Iron Man magazine. Just being in her presence made you take a look at yourself and ask the question, what do I have to do to look like that? She had a deep voice, and she was clean looking and extremely confident. She wasn't cocky though, she was pleasant to be around.

Stephanie had multiple cell phones which rang while we were in the lobby. I overheard her conversation at one point, it sounded like she ran a dating service. We all sat down to talk for a while. They chatted about the marathon and places to visit in Baltimore. Larry and I chatted with them also for a period of time. We talked about our lives and how different they turned out than we originally thought they would.

I told the girls goodnight and headed to the room for a good night''s sleep. Larry was amused by Stephanie's body, he kept asking her if she had ever taken steroids. Along the way, I yelled Larry come on, and he followed me to the elevator. We got on the elevator, and the door closed, I wanted to laugh but Larry kept talking about how muscular Stephanie was, and if I kept that conversation going he would never let me go to sleep.

We got to the room and I jumped into bed with my

clothes on. While trying to fall asleep I was thinking about superstitions that athletes indulge in right before a game. Most have some type of ritual they follow. They believe if they follow these rituals it will bring them good luck. It's usually something they say or do before their event. Some say this is a coping method for athletes who face excessive pressure to succeed.

Michael Jordan would always wear his UNC shorts under his NBA shorts, and Brian Urlacher would eat two chocolate chip cookies before every game. Tiger Woods wears a red shirt while competing in Sunday's golf tournaments. Babe Ruth always made sure he would step on second base whenever he jogged in from right field and if he forgot it he would run out from the dugout and kick it before the next half-inning began. Wade Boggs would field exactly 150 ground balls in the infield, start his batting practice at exactly 5:17 PM, and then run wind sprints at exactly 7:17 in pre-game practice. I wished I had some ritual to share but I don't, I just wake up, put on my headphones and run. Of course, I'm not under extreme pressure to win, I only have to beat myself but sometimes beating my self takes planning and execution. Fighting my will to lay on the couch all day, and do nothing. Getting up, putting on my shoes and walking out the door for a run when no one is around to motivate me. Now that's a tough row to hoe.

Before I knew it I fell asleep, I rolled on my stomach for a good night's rest. Larry has this thing when he sleeps, he has been doing it since we were kids. I call it the alligator roll. He rolls around in circles all night long. I'm surprised he's not tired when he wakes up. I looked it up years ago, scientists have a name for behavior like that while you sleep. They call it parasomnia.

Parasomnia is abnormal behavior that occurs during sleep. According to David Neumeyer, MD, a sleep specialist, "these behaviors can be kind of weird and scary." All I know is even to this day when I wake up and see him doing it (the alligator roll) it scares the hell out of me.

I woke up to pounding on the door. It was the girls screaming come on guys, today's the day. I yelled for Larry to wake up, he rolled over and said let's get breakfast before we put on our running clothes. In just seconds we were out the door and at the breakfast bar. I looked at the clock on the wall and it said 5 AM.

Looking at the breakfast bar I was thinking about eating eggs and bacon but I thought I would continue to carb-load to see for myself if it made a difference. I had pulled up an article by Dimity McDowell titled The Right Way to Carb-Load Before a Race.

McDowell said, "carbs are stored as glycogen in the muscles, and they are your body's most accessible form of energy, but not the only source. During the race, your body burns glycogen and fat. Fat takes a lot more work to convert into fuel. When you run out of glycogen during a race you hit the wall. Your body has to slow down until it turns your fat into fuel so you can keep going. That's why you see runners falling before the finish line. They struggle to get up and move forward. They are out of glycogen, and in the process of converting fat into energy." He also said you can't carb-load up in just one meal. "You need several meals to pack your muscles with glycogen, and with every gram of carbohydrates you store, you store 3 grams of water. This means your body will be hydrated and fueled to run your race."

I loaded up a pile of pancakes on my plate topped with jelly, and got a large glass of juice. I sat down next to the window to eat, hoping no one would see me scarf down a plate of food. Larry and Myra were sharing a plate of desire, as they were feeding each other breakfast. Courtney and Stephanie must have been overloaded with carbs because they were skateboarding across the lobby, and Patti was out front contributing a little portion to global warming with her hand-rolled cigarettes. I saw other people were performing rituals hidden to the untrained eye, most were just away from home, enjoying the moment, trying to check off another marathon.

Larry and I ran up to change for the marathon. We put on our clothes and pinned our bib numbers on the front of our shirts. We headed down to meet with the rest of the crew in the lobby. We were surprised to see Courtney's sister Morgan. She had her bib number on, she was ready to run. When she turned around I noticed that she had her dog in a K9 Sport Sack strapped to her back. I looked closer and saw a bib number on the dog's collar. It made me laugh. For a moment it had me thinking it was real.

Morgan got up early and drove down to Baltimore this morning. She planned on running the marathon but had to work late the night before. Morgan was 23 years old. She just graduated from Ohio State University. She was about 5 foot 5 inches tall and had brown hair. Morgan didn't play any sports in high school but often played football and basketball with her siblings in the summer. She was more an academic person than an athlete. She came for the social buzz and to spend time with her sister. Patti's kids finally arrived, so we all decided to walk down to the starting line together at the Harbor, it's a good mile or two but it's a good way to warm up before a run.

Morgan and Courtney were talking about the bib numbers. Courtney said they have a strip attached to the back of them, which allows them to track you as you run the marathon. They also have an app so your friends and family can see where you are in the race. You can send out a shout or cheer during the race to someone you know.

Stephanie said look at your bib, they have different colors at the bottom. The color identifies the wave you are in at the starting line. Patti said I didn't even notice. How do we know where a wave is located at the starting line? Stephanie said they have flags with your colors by the side of the starting line. Just stand in the color zone that matches the color on your bib. Everyone started yelling out their color, purple, violet, orange, green, and gold. I looked at my bib and it was hard to tell if it was yellow or gold. Stephanie looked at it and said it's gold and we are in the same wave. Larry was in Courtney's wave, and Patti was in Myra's wave.

WILLIAM CRAMER

Chapter 4

As we walked to the Harbor others joined in, they appeared from buildings, side streets, and cars. We were all walking in the same direction, toward the Harbor. It looked like a scene from The Walking Dead. It drew most of us to silence because of the mass.

Courtney and Stephanie didn't feel the same way as they were screaming and shouting all the way there. When we arrived there were a lot of runners at the starting gate. Most were just stretching and talking but there was a huge crowd waiting to go to the bathroom at the Porta Potties. There must have been 20 Porta Potties with long lines.

An announcer introduced a marathon legend who spoke to the crowd about his running career. When he was finished talking they announced that you have 5 minutes left before the race starts.

Runners started getting ready for the race, they took off the extra stuff that kept them warm and headed toward their assigned section. Some were still talking as if they didn't hear the 5-minute announcement.

I know this sounds odd but I couldn't stop thinking about the long lines at the Porta Potties. What will happen when the bell rings to start? Will those runners still be standing in line or will they join in with us and start running?

A middle-aged man was standing in front of me, I hadn't noticed him before but I glanced at him and noticed he only had one leg. The other limb had a prosthetic leg made for runners. Another affirmation that there are those in life who have faced some tragedy, and keep on going as though their life hasn't missed a beat. He truly was one of those persons.

I was blessed with his presence, and at that moment he inspired me to do more than just beat my self, I wanted to do the best that I was capable of doing. The one-minute announcement was made, and all the marathoners started to face the starting line. I noticed that our gold section was fuller and there was less room to move around than others.

Stephanie appeared next to me. She said Courtney and Larry were in the 2nd wave behind us, and Myra, Patti and Morgan were in the 4th wave. I looked and waved but could only see Larry.

The bell rang and we all took off running at a fast pace.

The group was tight at first but within a few hundred feet it started to spread out some. I looked back to see what happened to all those runners at the Porta Potties, some were still waiting in line, but most had jumped in a wave and joined the other runners.

I saw Dorothy running. I had completely forgotten about her. I started to run in her direction, on the other side of the street. She was making friends on the street, talking to others around her while she ran. I decided to hang back and observe her, she looked so different compared to the first time I met her.

I heard Larry yell out wait for me Cramer. I turned around and I saw Larry trying to keep up with Myra as she blew by me. Larry ran up to my right side and he said I can't keep up with Myra. That's exactly what I told you at the elevator yesterday. Just cuz someone is not as tall as you doesn't mean that they can't keep up with you. I looked at him and laughed, stop talking about yourself and look over there. Dorothy is running and making friends. Larry said I see her. She looks like she has done this before, and she is fast.

Just then Dorothy ran into a shop that was offering free subs for runners during the marathon. I said to Larry, well that's the last of Dorothy. We're not going to see her again. Larry said maybe she was hungry this morning and didn't have any food to eat. I bet you that we will see her again. She doesn't seem like the type of person that would give up. I think she is the type of person that just needs to be reminded that she is strong. All of us need to be reminded that we can achieve our dreams if we will just not give up.

Larry, I'm glad you said that because we all get in a rut at times and we need each other to remind us who we really are. Larry pulled back his shoulders and said thanks, Cramer.

Larry continued to say there are a lot of people from Baltimore that are standing on the street and sidewalks cheering us on during the run. I said most of them are standing in front of their houses. Some were dressed in costumes and others had made huge signs. Some played musical instruments, singing songs to the runners. It was amazing to see all the entertainment that came out to motivate us.

We were at our first-mile mark and people were still passing us up. I was afraid to look back, I thought we might be in the back of the pack. Just then Larry said to me look there is Dorothy, she is eating a sub and running.

I looked over at her while she was taking a bite of her sub, lettuce and some juices were falling from her face. She was keeping up with us though. She would take a couple of bites while chewing and swallowing her food. Then she would wrap the sub back up, and stick it back in the front of her pants. You could see lettuce all over her shirt and shorts.

Larry and I stopped paying attention to the runners in front of us, Dorothy became the focal point of the moment. As funny as it looked, I couldn't laugh. She pulled the sandwich out and repeated her eating process several times until it was finished.

I tried to refocus on the run but Larry spoke up and said she has another sub. I looked over and there she was unwrapping another sub preparing to take a bite. She was still keeping up with us, in fact her pace had picked up and she would soon pass us up. I was trying to process all of this when Larry said she had one more sub stuffed in the back of her pants.

Larry has always been my hero because he makes me laugh, but when he said that, I said that's not funny. He said I'm serious, she has one more sub stuffed in the back of her pants.

I looked over at Dorothy as other runners kept getting in

my way, trying to see that sub stuffed in her pants. I kept looking forward, then to the right, backward, then to the left. Suddenly I saw the sub, stuffed in the back of her pants. I said I can't believe it's there, you're not joking around Larry. No one will ever believe us if we tell them that a girl running a marathon had a sub stuffed in her pants.

Larry said Dorothy was his kind of girl, she's not afraid to eat in public that's for sure, and she doesn't care what other people think. She is the kind of person we need at the dealership. We both laughed and started moving her way, and when we arrived she smiled with food all over her mouth and said hey boys I'm so glad to see you. Then she took another bite of her sub. I had to look away, it was one of those moments where you have to think before you say or do anything. I wanted to laugh but I didn't know how she would take it. I couldn't avoid doing nothing. It was one of those situations where I usually laugh. Then that person gets offended and I end up looking like a jerk. I turned my head back around holding back my laugh as long as I could, then Larry spoke up and saved the day.

Larry looked at her and said jokingly, do you got any food? Dorothy pulled a piece off of the sub she was eating and handed it to Larry. The handoff looked professional. It looked like a first and ten to go handoff. There were no flags, no fouls, and no fumbles.

Larry just stared at the sub, the lettuce was dangling from side to side. The turkey meat was flapping front to back, and mayonnaise and ketchup were dripping on Larry's shirt. It seemed like a long time before Larry took a bite, but after he took one, the handoff back to Dorothy was also smooth. It was hilarious, all three of us were laughing because Larry was discombobulated.

Dorothy pulled some lettuce from her sandwich and threw it on Larry's shirt, I thought it would fall to the ground but it stuck, and I glanced over at the shirt. The design was definitely a Picasso. Picasso had a style called the Blue Period, then the Circus/Rose period. Larry was sporting the Green/Red period then the Circus/Lettuce period. Larry was always as neat as a priest handing out communion. I took a picture of him with my phone so I could sell it to the highest bidder at the dealership. I'm sure that picture could bring some dough.

Dorothy said I got to go guys, I need to get to the finish line. She ran off ahead of us with her sub smashed in her pants, and Larry and I started to focus again on the marathon.

We were on the second mile, Larry asked me if I had seen Myra since the race started. I said that I had not seen her since we walked to the Harbor this morning. Larry pulled out his phone, he pushed a couple of buttons and a red dot appeared. I asked Larry, what are you doing? Larry said I'm tracking Myra, I have her bib number and it shows me where she is at during the marathon. She is up ahead about a half of mile, let's see if we can catch her. Larry and I picked up the pace, we were running about a 9-minute mile.

Tracking runners is usually for family or friends, so they can see your progress during the marathon. Who would have thought to track their girlfriend during the same race so you would know if she is ahead or behind you? It sounds ingenious, why didn't I think of that.

We noticed some runners had stopped by the side of the road for a minute to rest, we didn't stop we kept on going. A group of people ran by us, and one of them was holding a sign in the air as he ran. It said one hour and forty-five minutes, he was a marathon pacer. If you wanted to finish in that time you had to keep up with them.

Larry and I admired them as they passed, but there was no way we would be able to keep up.

WILLIAM CRAMER

Chapter 5

It's hard to believe but there is a lot of conversation going on while you're running a marathon. The first competition race I ran I saw a lot of runners holding conversations during the race. Friends talking to each other while they were running, women chatting about their kids, and older people asking bystanders how much further it is to the finish line.

There was a large group of women and men up ahead in a tight formation. They were gossiping away, and they looked like they just joined the run. I said to Larry look at them, do you see any sweat on them? Do you see any signs that they are running a marathon except the bib?

Larry laughed. He said, where have you been Cramer? It's the gossip group.

The gossip group is no longer in the parlor sipping tea, they are in the street, in the church, on the soccer field, in the grocery store, they're everywhere. They're not here for the run, they're here to recruit young talent, to help them sharpen and perfect their gossiping skills.

Larry kept talking as we ran by them, I couldn't hear much of what he was saying. I stared at them as we ran by as if they were from a different planet. One person would talk, and the others would just nod their head in agreement. They would make faces of disappointment and chant things under their breath.

I could feel their force, it was strong, I felt like I was being pulled in, so I yelled Larry help me. Larry said I told you not to look at them. They will suck you into their web. Larry gave me a push and laughed, I laughed too, thinking crap, I knew they existed but I didn't know they were that organized.

We passed the 3-mile mark, and up until now, my body had been fighting the run. Everyone is different. Some say 2 miles, some 4 miles before their body is ready to go. A lot of people never experience the point at which the body yields because they give up. If and when they experience that feeling, they will feel empowered, because they are able to perform at a higher level than usual.

Madeline Buxton, who writes for Fitness Magazine, says, "To have a strong mental game is just as important as being physically fit. Multiple studies have looked at how mental toughness can boost your performance inside and outside of sports. Pros talk about training their brains using visualization techniques and mindful meditation."

Those are worth looking into if you get to the point where you want to make changes in your life that you have not been able to do in the past. I know for myself that seeing these changes has empowered me not only in my ability to run further but in my personal goals as well. You don't have to be stuck in the place you're at in your life. You can change the direction of your life, as tough as it seems, you just need to start by setting small goals each day, and completing them. The mental game starts now, you must choose to try or not.

We just turned the corner, we could see a large lake ahead. There was a large track that went completely around the lake. We could see runners running around the lake on the track. It looked like it was about two miles around. We passed the 4-mile mark, and my body was feeling good. I felt like I could run forever, and surprisingly Larry was keeping up. It was a good time to look for Courtney and Myra, they were ahead of us but not far. There must have been hundreds of people running around the lake.

Scanning the runners I saw Courtney, she is tall and I yelled out to Larry there is Courtney, Myra can't be far away. Larry picked up the pace some and I kept up. We were gaining on them, they were about a half a mile away. We moved through the crowd swiftly. Larry's long legs made it easy for him to run fast. All those runners that passed us by at the beginning of the race were now falling behind. We were passing them up right and left.

There were some residential homes on the right side of the road. It seems like we left the city limits and entered into a residential area. There was a shed near the road, it looked like a place for kids to wait for the school bus. It wasn't big at all. It was about four feet wide and three feet deep.

A young man ran around the right side of the shed to take a pee, at the same time a young lady noticed the shed and took off for the left side to take a pee. The young man was peeing when the young lady ran around the left side of the shed and ran into him. She then pulled down her pants and started peeing. The young man turned away and continued peeing.

It's not that everyone stopped to watch, it's just that when people run off into someone's yard during a marathon, you wonder where they are going. Now I'm not a big fan of believing things happen by coincidence but it happened. I have to ask myself what are the chances of two people of opposite genders having to pee at the same place at the same time. In the grass less than 9 feet apart, and they never met each other. All you math people can use an algebraic equation with x's and y's to figure out the chances of that happening, but how about we just say slim to none.

Larry yelled out, there is Myra just a few feet behind Courtney, I looked but couldn't see her. By now we were only a hundred feet away. We were almost around the lake, so I glanced back to see how far we came and I noticed Stephanie was on our tail. Patti was right behind her. She looked like she was just keeping up.

I turned back around and Larry said we are going to turn right up ahead. Everyone started slowing down as there was a huge crowd in front of us. It was caused by too many people trying to crowd in a small space at the same time. It was a strip that the marathon sponsors use to help track your location during the race. We crossed a few of them earlier but this strip was on a turn which made it awkward.

As we turned right we started downhill. I could see a water station up ahead with some Porta Potties on the side of the street. The temptation is to keep running and not stop. Thinking that you can make up some time but your body needs the carbs and liquids that these stations have to offer.

I stop at these stations and I refuel my body. I walk and

rub my legs, it keeps them from cramping up at the end of the race when you are pushing to finish. Think of it as a pitstop during the Daytona 500 where the race cars come to get water, new tires and fuel. These water stations hand out water, Gatorade, energy gel and energy chews.

Christine Luff wrote an article on the 10 best energy gels, chews and bars that was published on Verywell Fit. She says, "A general rule of thumb is to take in about 100 calories after an hour of running, and then another 100 calories every 40-45 minutes after that."

She also said, "Most sports gels contain 100 calories so it's easy to keep track how many calories you're consuming. Clif Shot Blocks energy chews are a great way to replenish the carbs and electrolytes your body needs. Gu Energy Gels are among the top picks for marathon runners because they're quickly and efficiently absorbed by your body."

When we got to the water station we saw Myra and Courtney refueling with liquids and gels. Larry went over to Myra to talk for a minute. Courtney laid down in the grass and started doing some crunches and sit-ups. I walked over to her and said are you OK? She just laughed and said I'm taking 5 to work on my 6-pack. Oh OK, that's cool, that must be important to you. She said it is one of my personal goals. I have a lot of goals and I'm always busy so I try to work on them in-between life events. I said that's so cool that you are focused even though your life is full of things to do. You still manage to reach your goals.

We seemed like we were at the water station forever but really it was less than a few minutes. We all got up and took off together. Larry, Myra, Courtney and I were running at a decent pace. Courtney was leading us, she was sweating but not as heavy as Myra.

Larry said something to Myra about her shirt being soaked, so she took it off and threw it on the side of the road. Yes, half of her designer outfit was lying on the side of the road. She was wearing a tank top underneath. Getting rid of that designer shirt seemed to help her cool down. It's not uncommon for runners to take clothes off and throw them on the side of the road when they're running a marathon. I have seen gloves, hats, shirts and sweatbands on the side of the road because they are not needed anymore and they just got tossed away.

When we got to the bottom of the hill we took a left. The road was brick and narrow, there were row homes on both sides of the road. People were sitting and standing in front of their homes, cheering us on. Some were holding signs, and others were looking for a high-five as we ran by them. They were really excited and full of energy. All that cheering makes you forget about the run for a short time and you begin to focus on the people cheering. As we ran through the streets I was thinking how good it was to be back together again with Myra and Courtney. We really didn't spend much time together before the race and here we are actually doing it, we are running a marathon together.

Myra yelled out, whoever loses has to buy us all supper tonight. Larry and Courtney yelled I'm in, once again it was a wrap before I got to say anything. Whoever had to pay the motel bill didn't matter to me, I just enjoyed their company and how we would challenge each other to move forward with our lives.

We were approaching the sixth-mile mark. The streets were so narrow at that point there was no room to pass other runners, so Courtney stepped up on the sidewalk and took off running. I followed her then so did Myra and Larry. The road opened up some so Courtney stepped back on the street again and continued to run. I noticed Courtney's running style, it was different from mine. She seemed to glide through the air without using a lot of energy. I asked her who taught you this running style? She looked at me and said, Coach Nate Helming.

He has a segment called The Run Experience. There's a segment that explains, "Nate's three steps to improve our foot strike are to first change our posture. We should stand up tall, connecting the line from the ears, shoulders, hips, knees to the ankles.

"As you start to run lead forward with the hips, not overextending the lower back. Posture is important because when you engage your hips, it extends your hips, opens them up so you have a hip extension, and as you run your stride opens up out of the back.

"Secondly, for every leg swing, there should be an arm swing, and thirdly cadence, active pulling with the hips. It helps recycle the movement a little faster and keeps your feet from dragging."

So I gave it a try, and it worked great. Larry said what are you doing Cramer? I said I'm learning how to run better than ever before. Larry laughed and said it's a marathon, don't you think you should practice that at home. I said why Larry, I have 7.1 miles to go to see if it works. Besides if it works you'll be buying supper for all of us, because Myra is in front of you, that makes you last.

We came across a warehouse building beside some row homes. The street was packed with spectators. There was a loading dock that faced the street, the dock set back a few feet from the street. There was no room for Courtney to step up on the sidewalk and pass so we just moved slowly with the others runners.

We were about to turn right, everyone was slowing down. I looked to the right at the loading dock, there were several homeless people there watching the race. Some were standing, some were sitting, and a few were lying down on the dock sleeping. I thought about Dorothy, I was wondering if they were some of her friends, if she dropped off those extra subs for them to eat. I guess I had slowed down too much because I felt a runner bump into me from behind. I looked over my left shoulder and it was someone that I didn't know, she said sorry dude, there is no room to run.

After we turned right we started downhill, the road was wider and there was more room. Courtney was weaving in and out passing runners. I felt like I was exceeding my normal pace, it was faster than I was used to. I wondered how long I would be able to last.

Courtney turned around and said there is a large group of people up ahead standing on the side of the road across from a water station. Let's get some water and see what's happening.

Chapter 6

As we got closer we could see someone had set up a karaoke station on the side of the street for people to stop by and sing. It was a large crowd, I guess it was over one hundred people. A marathon runner jumped up on stage tossing her drink to the side. She grabbed a mic, held up her hands, wiping the sweat from her face. She looked at the crowd and said my name is Emily Hunt. The music started playing, I knew the song well, it was I Will Survive by Gloria Gaynor. I guess this was her debut for glory in the middle of a marathon. We took in some gel packs and water as we turned around to listen to Emily make personal history.

Her voice was powerful, several runners stopped to listen. I closed my eyes for just a bit to take in the moment. When she finished everyone clapped, she bowed in gratitude, then she ran back into the crowd of runners and disappeared. We looked at each other and said that was awesome, then Courtney said OK peeps, its time to rumble. I took a sip of my water and jammed a gel pack down my throat, and we were off running again.

I had been thinking about running around the lake a few miles back, it was so difficult. I thought about Stephanie and Patti. Where were they? They were right behind us at the lake. We had stopped for water, twice, and to listen to Emily Hunt at the karaoke station, but we didn't see them.

I yelled out to Larry and Myra, did either of you see Stephanie or Patti lately? Myra said Patti was taking a smoke break while we were listening to Emily. They took off ahead of us, they didn't stay for the entire song. Courtney said she would look for them up ahead.

While we were running through the next intersection a cop was giving runners a high five and redirecting traffic at the same time. I hadn't stopped to thank any of the police for the excellent work they were doing redirecting traffic away from the marathon. It seemed that they were at every intersection, I was impressed with their service. It was top notch. When we got to the next intersection I ran by an officer and gave him a fist pound. He said to keep up the good work man. Larry just looked at me and laughed.

I told Larry that maybe it looked kind of corny, it even felt that way but I just wanted to acknowledge their presence and hard work. I felt it was the best way to express that at the moment. Next time I think I'll just yell out and say thanks. Larry said that's cool but I did get a picture of you giving that cop a fist pound. It looks awkward too. Maybe I can trade it for that photo you took of me earlier when I was eating the sub with Dorothy.

This is why Larry is the top salesman, he is a skilled negotiator. I said OK Larry let me think that over for a bit.

Courtney stepped up on the curb again, and we followed her. There was an ambulance ahead in the way. They were working on a runner for some reason. We didn't stick around to find out. All the runners slowed down and some stopped on the street. We stepped around and continued to run at a good pace.

I heard a cell phone ring, then another phone rang. I knew that Stephanie must be close, so I looked around but I didn't see her anywhere. We started downhill again, I looked ahead and it seemed like a long way to the bottom.

I was focusing on my running style when someone tapped me on the back and said in a deep voice; could you move over a bit, there is a blind man coming up on your left side.

Myra heard him say that also and she said Cramer did you hear him, there is a blind man coming up to your left. I turned my head to the left and there was a man in front of the blind man warning others like me that a blind man was coming by them. On the right side of the blind man was a woman holding a piece of string, the blind man was holding the other end. The string was tight between the two. It looked like she was guiding him with it. There were three other people, one on either side of the blind man and one man behind them all, that made a team of five for the blind man including the woman holding the string.

Myra moved close to me so she could get a look at the blind man running the marathon. She stared at him for a while. It got to the point that it was uncomfortable so I said to Myra what's wrong? She said he really is blind. I said it looks that way, and it also looks like we are going to be passed by a blind man in a half-marathon. I thought about how I have never been exposed to blind athletes before in my entire life.

Myra said, I just read an article on Erik Weihenmayer. He went blind at age 14, diagnosed with retinoschisis. He graduated from college, became a teacher, he summited Mount Everest, did the Seven Summits, climbing each continent's highest mountain, wrote 3 books, was on the cover of Time Magazine, and currently helps visually impaired children learn how to climb.

I said wow, I think that most people have low expectations for people that are blind. Myra said that's what is so interesting about this man, he is doing a half-marathon, and that's huge. I said to Myra, hold my hand for a minute let me experience what's it's like to run blind.

Myra grabbed my hand and I ran with her holding my hand a few hundred feet. I opened my eyes and Myra said what did it feel like? I said I had a hard time keeping my balance, I felt like I was going to fall over. I was trying to use my other senses but it was difficult. I felt alone even though I heard other people talking. I felt insecure.

Myra said let me try it, so I held her hand for a few hundred feet while she ran. When she opened her eyes a tear ran down the side of her face. I said, what's wrong?

She said we take so much for granted each day. I was complaining this morning when I got up because my makeup didn't go on right. I'm glad this man ran by us. I needed this experience to realize how good I really have it. I get so busy doing stuff, that I don't take the time to appreciate the things I have in my life.

Courtney overhearing the conversation, slowed down to talk. She said there was a blind teen from Minnesota that completed an Ironman Triathlon in Louisville last year. His name was Louie McGee and he completed it in twelve hours and fifty-eight minutes. He is an incredible athlete and he gives back to others. He runs a non-profit called Louie's Vision where he helps youth through mentoring and events.

Wow, I would like the opportunity to meet them someday but for now it would be nice to have some of their books in our school so the students can learn about these incredible lives.

Courtney shouted come on guys, it's time to go. Let's show Louie we can do it too. A group of marathon pacers holding a sign that said two hours ran by us. Courtney said we should try to pace ourselves with them and run behind them. Courtney was getting tired so Myra and Larry took the lead. Myra is short but don't let her designer outfit fool you, that girl can run. I was worried about Larry, I didn't want him to fall behind. I didn't want him to distract Myra.

Soon we started running up a hill again, and there were a lot of runners falling behind. The street was full of runners so Myra and Larry stepped up on the sidewalk and started running around them. The only difference this time was that the sidewalks were crowded with spectators who came to cheer us on, which made it difficult for Larry and Myra. Courtney ran behind me for a mile or two. I could tell that she was getting tired. We were going on our ninth mile, and it looked like she needed a rest.

I was looking for a place to pull over and stop for a moment because I didn't want her to get to the place I was at during my first run event. The first time I ran in a competition race I vowed not to stop. I ended up struggling at the end of the race just to finish. My energy levels were down and my legs were cramped so bad I had to do the shuffle to finish. I almost didn't make it.

We were heading around a small park, and I could see the runners on the other side. I heard a dog barking and thought nothing of it until I saw Morgan and Stephanie. Morgan was walking her dog, after all, it had been in that K9 Sport Sack for some time. I guess it got too heavy for Morgan because Stephanie had the sack strapped to her back.

I said to Larry there is not much time to walk a dog while you're running a marathon. I know people are emotionally attached to their pets. I had a girlfriend that had a small dog. It bit me 3 times and tore my pants one time. When I told her and confronted her about it she said that you guys are going to have to work it out. I asked her what does that mean, we need to work it out? Does it mean we need to sit down together and negotiate the space we are sharing? If we can't reach an agreement we can just bite each other. Larry laughed and said well, did you work it out. Ya, I moved out of the house.

Larry and Myra laughed. Larry said Cramer that's Morgan's good luck charm, she actually believes when she talks the dog understands what she is saying. I saw them at breakfast, she was asking the dog what he wanted for breakfast by pointing at it. The dog would bark and then she would put that food on the plate.

I said I guess I missed it all being seated by the window. Well, you missed a lot, do you even know his name? Not really, I heard Courtney mention it but I forgot. Well, his name is Bentley. You mean like Bentley Motors, yes exactly. That's funny, she named him after a car manufacturer. Larry, did you ever see their company logo? It's a capital B with wings on each side. Larry said B is alphabetically close to the top of the list. She didn't make it to the R's for Rover. There were probably so many names she stopped at the B's.

We all stopped at the water station and then walked across the street to chat with Morgan and Stephanie for a minute. Larry said I needed a break, we were on our 9th mile. I picked up a few gel packs for Courtney and handed them to her. I said take these, they will give you energy and help you make it to the end of the race. This is the hard part of the half-marathon. You have 4 miles left and you're tired.

I told Larry to grab some gel packs too, you have to keep up with Myra, and you didn't look like you were doing so good the last mile. He went over and grabbed 5 gel packs and some water. He cracked them open and down they went with a smile. I said Larry you only need one or two, we're not doing a triathlon today.

Morgan loaded up Bentley on Stephanie's back and we all took off. We now had six people in our group running and talking, we kind of looked like the gossip group. Larry was in front, Myra was second, I was behind Courtney. Morgan and Stephanie were behind me. Myra reminded us four, and told the two who hadn't heard it before, whoever loses will have to pay for everyone's meal. They all agreed, even the dog barked.

We took off and eventually caught up with the two-hour pace group. It's hard to keep up with where everyone is during the race. Someone may start out behind you but when you make a stop they may pass you unnoticed. It's hard to keep track of those in your group, unless you're Larry.

Morgan and Stephanie had pulled in front of us without me noticing it. I have no idea where Dorothy is at this point. In fact where's Patti at in this race?

I yelled out to Stephanie when is the last time you saw Patti? Stephanie said Patti kept running when we stopped at the park. She said she wanted to get a head start because she didn't want to finish last. She will stop for a smoke break, hopefully we will be able to catch up to her soon. OK everyone look for Patti along the way, she may be taking a break along the road.

At this point I'm not sure out of our group who will be first or last. However when it gets close to the end of the race, I will not be last. I have been preparing for this race for some time. Mr. Ruffin had sent me a running plan for a half-marathon. I had been following the plan most of the time. Ruffin's eating is clean so I thought I'd start eating clean like him.

Chapter 7

We are finally heading back to the Harbor with the last 4 miles to go. Larry was out front and I noticed that he was distracted by some cars that were for sale on the side of the road. Up until this point Larry had not glanced at one car for sale, he didn't have time to think about it, he was distracted by everything else. Now that he was out front and leading everyone, he had time to think about cars, especially cars for sale.

Larry has this thing for cars, he will stop in the middle of doing something just to look at a car. I can't tell you how many times we were in his car together and made a U-turn just to look at a car for sale. I have spent hours along the side of the road waiting for him. I didn't want that to happen here while we were running a marathon.

I thought I would head his distraction off by yelling out to him, Hey Larry can we kick it up a little, I want to finish strong. He didn't say a word or look back. I thought he didn't hear me, so I said it again, Larry can we move a little faster, I want to finish strong. This time he responded with hey Cramer, look at these cars for sale along the street. I would love to have some of them on my lot. Larry, please don't think cars right now, we need you out front thinking about keeping a decent pace.

Larry said OK Cramer I got this, don't worry about me. We went about 4 blocks and I noticed Larry running closer to the cars on the side of the street than before. Every once in a while he would see a car with a for sale sign on it and he would slow down to see what it looked like inside. It got to the point that the two-hour group was pulling away from us and I had to think of something to do before we came to a screeching halt.

We ran a few more blocks, I turned around and asked Stephanie and Morgan if they would take the lead. They said sure, and they moved up to the front of our group and sent Larry back to talk with me.

Larry came back and we started to talk about the finish line. We talked about Dorothy, we talked about the directions I scratched on my hand so I wouldn't get lost during the marathon. I thought somewhere along the way I would be the only one running and I needed directions, boy was I wrong. All you really have to do is follow everyone else. With the number of runners that sign up for these events, you will never be by yourself unless you're in last place.

We had just passed a sign for 10 miles and Morgan was getting tired, I asked her if she thought she was going to make it and she said yes. Larry reached into his pocket and pulled out a gel pack and gave it to Morgan to eat. She opened it, and down it went. He gave her another one, and down that one went also. It seemed to help her some. She picked up her pace a little. I said, Larry, how many of those packs did you get? Larry said I just grabbed a handful.

We took a right and headed down another street with bystanders on the sidewalks holding up signs. What is the motive behind these signs anyways? Some are funny and some make no sense. I think that it's their way of connecting with their community, but some signs are more than that, it seems that they are seizing an opportunity to advertising for themselves.

Like the lady that was dressed up in a wedding gown standing on the sidewalk with a sign saying, "Looking for one good man." It looked like the Uncle Sam poster that says looking for a few good men. I guess it worked for Uncle Sam, it may work for her too. I will give her an A for effort because she is not looking in the usual places. She is looking for a healthy active man who is able to reach some goals instead of just talking about it, and that's heavy, man.

I said Larry, look over your right shoulder, so you can see who is about to pass you up. Do you remember him from the elevator? I bet he remembers you cuz he is looking right at your back. That's the last thing he saw as he passed you face down in front of the elevator.

Larry said oh crap, it's the ten-year-old. He looks like he is tired though. Larry, we are all tired we have been running over an hour. Myra said to Larry what happened in the elevator, Larry said I'll tell you when it's convenient. It's hard not to laugh, with his dry humor you don't know if he is goofing around or serious.

We continued to keep up with the two-hour pace group, but that boy from the elevator passed them up and kept on going. I'm not sure what his final time would be but I would guess that it will be better than ours. We were passing a big church on the left. It looked like it had been there for some time. They had a huge gate, and it was open. There were a lot of gravesites that went all around the church. I thought the church was closed until a man walked out of the front doors and down to the street. He was holding some flyers, so I yelled out to him can I have one of those flyers. He yelled out sure so I ran by him and picked up a flyer and kept running.

Stephanie said do you know who is buried there? I said no but it must have been a long time ago, cuz all those grave sites are old. She said Edgar Allan Poe, and that man gives tours of the grounds during the week. I said really, after the run I'm going to stop back because we are doing Edgar Allan Poe in English class and I would love to have some new information about him. Morgan yelled out that he was the first author to try to make a professional living as a writer, and much of Poe's work was inspired by the events that happened around him.

Wow, cuz he writes some dark stuff like The Masque of the Red Death. Courtney spoke up and said where do you think he got the idea for that story? Larry said the man definitely tells the story like he was there himself.

Just then we saw Patti running up ahead. Stephanie yelled out to her to wait up but she couldn't hear her. We all moved over to the left side of the road to catch up to her but she was kicking everyone's tail.

Stephanie said Patti was sick two years ago, she is Irish and she went to Ireland and kissed the Blarney Stone. She came back healed of her sickness. She believes that it was the rock that healed her.

Myra said for over 200 years people have been kissing that rock to gain the gift of eloquence. We all have our own beliefs about things that bring us luck and healing. I'm glad she is healed but I hope she slows down soon.

We have three miles left to reach the finish line, and I'm not sure that I can keep this pace up for that long. This is like a full sprint. Larry said all we need is someone to strike up a band, and we will be at this speed all the way to the finish line.

When we hit the eleventh mile, we were passing up a lot of runners, and we finally caught up with Patti. Stephanie got close to her to see if she was OK. Patti said I'm fine, but I can't wait to get to the finish line. Stephanie still had Morgan's dog on her back, and it would bark now and then. He was on the same page as Patti, let's get to the finish line now. No one really said it but I shouted it out to let everyone know that we have stuck together through most of the race but when we get to the last mile it's everyone for himself.

I didn't get much of a response but what was I expecting? Everyone had already decided to make it to the end but didn't wanna shout it out. Well, I felt stupid, I felt the same way when I high-fived the cop a couple miles back. Sometimes we repeat the mistakes we already made, and I have to say, what's that all about.

Patti slowed down some and I think we all were relieved. I think we all needed to breathe for a moment before we made the dash to the finish. I'm good with a one-mile dash to the finish but more than that and I will be flopping around on the ground gasping for air.

Courtney shouted out hey guys here is Emily Hunt. Myra and Larry both said to her, you have an awesome voice, where did you learn to sing like that Emily. She said I have been singing since I was ten years old. I entered some contest but I was not able to move forward with my talent. Wow someone dropped the ball because your performance was awesome.

Emily looked like she was in her forties. She was very attractive. She had dark skin and black hair. She said when she was young she had other obligations that kept her from moving forward. She said I regret it and wish I could go back to that day I decided not to proceed with my singing career but I can't, its too late.

Myra shouted out to Emily after we finish the race stop by and see me, I have some connections in the music industry. I'm staying at the Holiday Inn Express by the Harbor. I will be there all weekend. Emily said thank you, I'll stop by in the morning.

I started moving over toward Larry, we had about a mile and a half left till we crossed the finish line. I said to Larry what do you want to do here, we only have a mile and a half left to go. We can't lose the race because we would have to pay for the motel rooms, remember the bet. Larry said he didn't know what to do when you get toward the end of the marathon. I said I have a strategy, actually, it's Jeff Gaudette's strategy. He says you need to "manage your pace to control your race."

It's a big article with a lot of facts but here's the skinny. Most marathoners run much faster in the first half of the race, and slower in the second half of the race, it's called putting the time in the bank. Jeff says when you do this your performance may be not what you need it to be when you get to the finish line. Basically, you're not going to finish strong.

A better strategy is maybe to start off slow (close to your goal time) in the first half and then speed up gradually in the second half so when you need that energy at the finish line it will be there, and ready to perform. You will have enough energy to finish strong.

I said to Larry, I like his idea, I don't want to run out of energy right before the finish line so here's what we can do. We have a mile and a half left. Let's speed up about 2 percent more than we are currently running for a half mile. Next we will kick it up 3 percent more for the next half mile, and finally the last half mile we will kick it up another 4 percent all the way to the finish line. It will be a gradual increase and we will be able to finish strong.

WILLIAM CRAMER

Chapter 8

I looked at Larry and said it's now or never, are you in or not? Larry shouted out I'm in let's go. I kicked it up about 2 percent and looked straight ahead. Larry followed right behind me. I could hear Stephanie's phones ringing as we started to move forward.

I looked ahead and I couldn't see the finish line. The road veers off to the left and after that we had to go down the hill past the museum to get to the finish line. I decided to speed up a little bit and I heard Larry let out a scream, it sounded like he was calling his ancestors for help. When I looked over my right shoulder to see if Larry was still there he pointed up ahead to the left. I looked but I didn't know what I was looking for at this point.

Then all of a sudden I picked out Courtney, Stephanie and Patti, running all out for the finish line. Larry shouted out run Cramer run. I yelled back, let's stick to the plan, they are not that far ahead, they are going to burn a lot of energy too early in the game and may not have it when they get close to the finish line. I looked over and Morgan's dog was barking. I guess he was talking to us but I didn't know what he wanted.

My thoughts were that he was saying goodbye guys, I'll see you both at the finish line.

At this point my body was feeling strong, my legs were not cramping up at all and my breathing was good. We made a left turn and I could see the finish line. We had a mile to go, so I kicked it up 3 percent more. I could see the girls up on the left. They were only 20 feet away from us and after kicking it up 3 percent we had begun to close the gap.

I have no idea why but Tim Allen's words pop up in my brain, from the movie Galaxy Quest where he is captain of a ship in outer space. He is in a galactic war with some space creature. During his fight with this beast he yells out "Never give in never give up." I don't know why but it inspired me and seemed to release a huge amount of energy.

As we approached the half mile we were even with the girls, I yelled to Larry we are going to kick it up another 3 percent all the way to the finish line. Larry didn't say a word so I glanced over my right shoulder to see what he was doing. Larry was huffing and puffing. Just like the big bad wolf in the cartoon of the Three Little Pigs. The wolf huffed and he puffed but he couldn't blow the last house down. Do you remember what the wolf's face looked like? Well, that's what Larry's face looked like.

I yelled out to Larry see you at the finish line. I could tell he was not going to be able to keep up. Courtney was keeping up but the other two had fallen behind. They were running out of energy, soon to hit the wall. Courtney and I were running flat out for the finish line. I could hear her making all kinds of noises. The next thing I knew my foot hit the finish line, and just a few seconds later Courtney shouted I made it.

I turned around to see where everyone was, and I saw Stephanie, Patti, Morgan and Larry cross over the finish line. We were all out of breath, we couldn't even talk to each other. I pointed over to the right about 20 feet, it was the recovery station. I motioned for us to go there.

Everyone started heading that way. We could hear others shouting as they crossed the finish line too. The recovery station is the one place that's closed off from the public. It's just for the marathon runners to come into after the marathon. They have tons of recovery food and drinks.

We all got in line for some refreshments and water. We picked up our finisher medals and we went over and sat down on the grass. We laid on the grass for about 10 minutes just taking in juices and fruit and looking at the blue sky, no one really said anything to each other. Patti lit up a cigarette, I could smell the smoke. Bentley was jumping all over everyone and he came over my way and jumped up on top of me.

I stood up to get away from him and I looked over and noticed Dorothy standing about 25 feet away talking to reporters. I said Larry Dorothy is over there, do you see her she's talking to some reporters, let go over there and see what's going on. We told the other girls, we will be back in a couple minutes. They were so tired that no one even responded. Larry and I headed over to see Dorothy.

WILLIAM CRAMER

Chapter 9

When we got over to where Dorothy was several reporters were asking her questions. She was telling a story, it was about her experience being homeless on the streets of Baltimore.

While we listened in she was telling the radio station about two guys that changed her life. I wondered who that was at first but we realized that she was talking about Larry and I. We listened for a while until she spotted us and called out our names. I'm not really a spotlight person. I love to help others but I am not good at taking credit for much. On the other hand, Larry loves the spotlight and he lives for taking credit for everything.

So when the radio station requested our presence on stage, we started walking in that direction. Larry dragged me up by my arm. I was trying not to look around as we walked up to the stage, but I glanced out at the crowd, and there were thousands of people watching the show. I glanced at the camera crew, and there were several local stations broadcasting this event. I even heard the girls give a shout out to Larry and I.

When we got up to the stage, Dorothy ran over to us and hugged us both. It was a long hug, you know what I'm talking about. The kind where you count to 15 and they're still hanging on with their arms wrapped around you. They say an average hug lasts 3 seconds, I guess I got a longer than average hug.

We stood beside Dorothy while she continued to tell everyone what we had done, and everyone clapped. I don't know who all the people were that came up on stage but they shook our hands and placed another medal around our necks. I looked over at the girls and they were clapping and shouting too. I asked if the girls could come up on stage with us and they said yes. A photographer took a group picture of all of us. Then someone stepped up to the mic and started talking with Dorothy.

When they were done, Dorothy came over to talk to us. I asked her for her real name. She said my name is Anna McKinley, and I have been homeless for some time. I use to have a marketing job traveling around the world until I lost it a few years back. I was so distraught that I gave up on life and started living on the street.

We introduced her to the girls and they all hugged her and asked her what she was going to do from this point on. Anna said the station offered to help her get back up on her feet by providing a place to stay and a job.

Larry and I gave her our phone numbers and said our goodbyes. We said if there is anything thing we can do to help you let us know. Anna thanked us and gave us both a kiss on the cheek.

The station provided a limo to take us back to the motel. Of course, the girls were yelling and screaming in the limo. They were having the time of their life. Some reporters rode back with us and continued to ask us questions. When we got to the motel and walked into the lobby, there were more reporters trying to ask us more questions. Larry rolled up his sleeves and answered several questions for a bit.

I went to the room to take a shower, and so did the girls. Then Larry came up and had a shower too. He said the limo was out front waiting to take us out to eat. He went over to the girls' room and told them about the limo and the girls started to scream even more. There was a man who rode with us in the limo, he stayed with us and paid for our meals and the motel bills when we returned back that night. We all agreed that it was the best night of our lives.

The next morning we got up early and went down for breakfast. We all sat close to each other and talked about the marathon and Anna McKinley. Emily Hunt stopped by and ate with us. After we ate, she and Myra stood up and sang a song together. It sounded awesome but Myra should stick to designing clothes. They exchanged phone numbers and said goodbye.

We loaded up the car and headed back home. On the way we talked about the run, all the things we saw along the way, we talked about our future goals and of course about running another marathon.

The girls were looking up the next marathon in our area. They shouted out Philadelphia. That's where we are going for our next marathon. It starts in 6 weeks, so guys start training. We laughed and said that sounds like fun, Larry and I will be ready. We finally pulled in my driveway and got out of the car.

The girls loaded their cars up with their luggage, and Larry kissed Myra goodbye.

I went to bed and started to look over some pictures that I took at the marathon. I was thinking about the whole trip.

Running a marathon was something that I had never done before. I have to say it again because you might have missed it the first time I said it. Stepping out and trying something new enriched my life. I was initially afraid when I first thought about doing it, but thanks to Mr. Ruffin, I managed to do it.

That week we met at the Brewery again. We all talked about our week. Larry sold more cars because of the publicity he received, Myra created a running outfit that was disposable. Courtney got a couple of new outfits for the gym. Stephanie created a new dating web site called Marathon Mingle, Patti got a new machine to roll up more cigarettes in less time, and I wrote this book.

THE MIGHTY MARATHON

WILLIAM CRAMER

Bibliography

Luff, C. (2018, December 22) The 10 Best Energy Gels, Chews and Bars to Buy for Running in 2019. Retrieved from: https://www.verywellfit.com/energy-gels-chews-and-bars-for-running-2911569

Buxton, M. (2019, January 24) What Actually Makes You Tired During Exercise. Retrieved from: https://www.fitnessmagazine.com/workout/cardio/tips/what-actually-makes-you-tired-exercise/

Giblin, C. (2019, January 22) 10 Most Interesting, Superstitious Rituals of Professional Athletes. Retrieved from: https://www.mensjournal.com/sports/10-most-interesting-superstitious-rituals-of-professional-athletes/

McDowell, D. (2018, June 12) The Right Way to Carb-Load Before a Race. Retrieved from: https://www.runnersworld.com/nutrition-weight-loss/a20826888/the-right-way-to-carbo-load-before-a-race/

Iliades, C. (2019, January 18) Odd Things People Do in Their Sleep. Retrieved from: https://www.everydayhealth.com/sleep-pictures/odd-things-people-do-in-their-sleep.aspx

Gaudette, J. (2012, October 18) Learn to Pace Like a Pro. Retrieved from: https://www.runnersworld.com/advanced/a20847773/learn-to-pace-like-a-pro/

Helming, N. (2016, October 17) Proper Running Footstrike. Retrieved from https://www.youtube.com/watch?v=Rt9hgtFzZk0

Weihenmayer, E. (2019, January 15) About Erik. Retrieved from: https://erikweihenmayer.com/about-erik/

About the Author

Will Cramer is the author of *The Mighty Marathon*.
He enjoys running in different parts of the country.
He runs half-marathons, Spartan obstacle races and enjoys
running with a local club. Will has a B.S. from Liberty
University in Business Administration and a Masters in
Education from East Stroudsburg University. Will has been
teaching students with disabilities for
the past 17 years.